Prouly

Cubs
All Alone

Cubs All Alone

Susan Hughes

Illustrations by Heather Graham

SCHOLASTIC CANADA LTD.
Toronto New York London Auckland Sydney
Mexico City New Delhi Hong Kong Buenos Aires

Scholastic Canada Ltd.
604 King Street West, Toronto, Ontario M5V 1E1, Canada

Scholastic Inc.
557 Broadway, New York, NY 10012, USA

Scholastic Australia Pty Limited
PO Box 579, Gosford, NSW 2250, Australia

Scholastic New Zealand Limited
Private Bag 94407, Botany, Manukau 2163, New Zealand

Scholastic Children's Books
Euston House, 24 Eversholt Street, London NW1 1DB, UK

www.scholastic.ca

National Library of Canada Cataloguing in Publication

Hughes, Susan, 1960-
Cubs all alone / Susan Hughes ; illustrations by Heather Graham.
(Wild paws)

Originally publ. 2004.

ISBN 978-0-545-98533-8

I. Graham, Heather II. Title. III. Series : Hughes, Susan, 1960- . Wild paws.
PS8565.U42C82 2009   jC813'.54   C2009-901187-5

ISBN-10 0-545-98533-1

6 5 4 3 2   Printed in Canada   121   14 15 16 17 18

MIX
Paper from
responsible sources
FSC® C004071

To Georgia's good friend, Erin Kainu.

Thank you to Sally Maughan, founder of the Idaho Black Bear Rehabilitation Center, for her expertise and thoughtful comments.

Contents

Chapter One

Help!

"Summer has almost come to Wild Paws and Claws, hasn't it, Nutcracker?" called out Max.

Ch-ch-ch-ch, the red squirrel nattered back at her from his enclosure. Max giggled. Nutcracker always seemed grumpy, even on sunny days like this one. Max drained his dish and carefully filled it with fresh water.

"Well, I can see that your grey belly is turning back to its summer white. And your red winter coat is turning orangey again," Max said.

Ch-ch-ch-ch, repeated Nutcracker. From within his tree hollow, he twitched his tail angrily. The blind red squirrel lived year-round at the wildlife centre. His pen was one of several in the forest clearing, all arranged in a semi-circle. One of Nutcracker's neighbours was Tippy, the three-legged red fox. In another pen lived two raccoons, Flora and Bandit. Flora's hind claws were damaged, and Bandit had lost an eye. None of these animals could survive in the wild, so Wild Paws and Claws had become their home.

"Goodbye, Nutcracker," sang out Max. "See you tomorrow." She headed down the pathway through the trees to the main office building.

When Max reached the isolation room at the back of the building, she stopped. The door was covered with photos of Tuffy the bobcat, and Max couldn't help but admire them. She pushed her brown bangs off her face and smiled at the very first photo, her favourite. It showed Tuffy as a tiny kitten. She was orangey-brown with little black and white spots. Her eyes were still closed. Because her ears were pressed back, the tufts on them didn't show.

Max sighed as she remembered meeting Tuffy for the first time. How the bobcat had mewed with hunger! How tiny she had been! Max had been so frightened that Tuffy wouldn't survive, but now she was one year old.

It had been a whole year since Max's family had moved to Maple Hill. Days later Max, her brother David, and their grandmother had found the orphaned bobcat in the woods and brought it to Wild Paws and Claws.

It had also been a whole year since Max had started at her new school and become best friends with Sarah. And it had been a whole year since the two girls had begun helping out at the centre.

Tuffy was still here, in the isolation room. She had an outdoor pen, too, but it was strictly off-limits to visitors. The bobcat had to be kept away from people so she wouldn't learn to trust them. If she was kept wild, she could one day be returned to the forest. Until then, Abbie, the owner of Wild Paws and Claws, still took a photo of Tuffy every month. That way visitors could see what she looked like, and how quickly she was growing.

"Daydreaming?"

Max turned at the sound of her friend's teasing voice. Sarah, wearing her usual jeans and a T-shirt, carried one empty bucket and one half-filled with birdseed. As she came nearer, Max pointed at the pictures on the door.

"You're thinking about Tuffy again," Sarah said. "Abbie wants to talk to us about releasing her."

"I know." Max managed a crooked smile. "Tuffy's now an expert at looking after herself. I'm sure she'll be able to survive in the wild on her

own. But . . . " she paused. "You know, it makes me happy to think of Tuffy being free, but I'm sad that I might never see her again."

"I feel the same way," Sarah admitted. "It'll be hard to say goodbye to her." She bit her lip, and twisted the end of a red braid around her finger.

Both girls cared so much for Tuffy. They loved all wild animals, and spent as much time as they could at Wild Paws. They worked there every week-end as tour guides, and they came by several days a week to help care for the permanent creature guests.

A year ago, the centre had almost closed because there wasn't enough money to run it. The girls had come up with a great idea. They helped prepare a special open house at the centre. People had come from far and wide, and lots of money had been raised. On Halloween, Max and Sarah had arranged a special spooky-evening event, with contests and treats. And at Easter they had decorated the centre with posters and streamers.

"When does Abbie think Tuffy can be released?" asked Sarah.

Max counted on her fingers. "Well, Tuffy can hunt on her own. She's more than six months old. She's afraid of humans. And the nice weather will help her get used to her new surroundings. Abbie said there's just one last thing that Tuffy needs. A vet has to look her over. If she's healthy . . . " Max swallowed. "She can return to the woods any day now."

Sarah frowned. "A vet. Hmm . . . "

Max nodded. This worried her. Wild Paws used to have a volunteer vet, Dr. Jacobs. But the elderly man had retired last year. Recently a veterinary student, Randall, had helped them with an injured snowshoe hare. But now he was away at university. Who could help them out with Tuffy? It didn't seem fair to keep her captive because they couldn't find a wild-animal vet to give her a check-up!

Just then, the girls heard a voice calling from the front of the office. It sounded like Abbie. "Girls! Come here, please. I need your help! Quickly!"

Max and Sarah looked at each another. Max knew that the same thought was flashing through both their minds. Was there another injured animal arriving at Wild Paws?

Chapter Two

The Law Allows It

The girls came rushing around the corner of the building and nearly bumped into Abbie.

"Oh, my!" the tall woman exclaimed. She held out one long arm to keep her balance, while the other went up to clutch at her round, owlish glasses and keep them from falling off.

"What is it, Abbie? What's wrong?" asked Max.

Abbie looked at the girls steadily. "This might take a moment. Why don't we all sit down on the steps while I explain?"

Max and Sarah were happy to rest their legs. The sun was shining but not too hot. It felt good on Max's face.

"I'm not sure how much you know about black bears," Abbie began, "but they live in many parts of North America, including this part of Canada."

Black bears? Max glanced at Sarah excitedly. She had never seen a black bear before. Was an injured black bear coming to Wild Paws? How big was it? Where would they put it?

Abbie caught Max's eye as she continued. "Most black bears are dormant for stretches of time in the winter. This means that their temperature drops a little bit, and their heartbeats slow down a lot. They doze for most of the winter months. They don't eat or drink. This is their way of surviving when there isn't much food."

"They sleep in dens, don't they?" Sarah asked.

"Usually," said Abbie. "And during the winter, mostly in January, mother black bears have their cubs. They nurse them and keep them warm through the winter while they doze. When the weather warms up, the bears come out to look for food. The mothers continue to nurse their babies for about six months. Meanwhile, they show them what's good to eat. They teach them how to be bears, and how to survive in the wild."

Max was interested in learning about black bears, but found it hard to concentrate. Was an injured black bear coming to Wild Paws? Otherwise, why would Abbie be telling them all this?

Abbie pressed her lips together. Her face looked grim. "When the bears come out of hibernation, it's spring. There isn't a lot to eat until the middle of July, when berries begin to ripen. So for months the bears are hungry and searching for food. Black bears are very shy and they usually keep away from humans. Except when they're hungry. Bears have a great sense of smell, and they can smell the grease left on a barbecue or garbage in a garbage can. If they're really hungry, they'll come on to people's property, looking for food."

Abbie paused again. She took off her glasses, wiped them and put them back on again. "And this bothers some people," she went on. "When they see a bear on their property, they might think the bear is dangerous, or maybe they just don't like to have the bear poking through their garbage night after night. They call it a 'nuisance bear.' If it comes back a few times, and the people think it's dangerous, they might trap it and have it removed. Or they might shoot the bear. The law allows it."

Max felt her stomach twist. Now she knew what this was all about. And she didn't like it. Not at all.

Abbie cleared her throat. "I just received a phone call from someone named Barton Crew. He says that a few days ago his neighbour shot and killed a black bear that was coming around his compost pile."

Max drew in her breath. She felt Sarah grip her hand.

"Mr. Crew is worried. He thinks it was a mother bear. There were two cubs, and he doesn't know what happened to them. He saw the mother's body being removed, but didn't see the cubs anywhere. He's hoping that we can go out and take a look."

Max said softly, "Oh, the poor things. Abbie, of course we'll go and look for them, won't we?"

Abbie smiled kindly. "Yes, of course we will. That's why I was coming to find you girls. The cubs will need our help. Their mom will have taught them to eat a few wild things, like plant roots and maybe ants. But they're not ready to survive on these things alone. They usually need to nurse until the end of July or so. They'll be hungry after a few days without Mom. So let's get going! You girls can get our usual rescue equipment, but remember to bring two large carriers, not just one. We'll also need the grab pole and the nets, too. I'll be with you in a moment."

Max and Sarah jumped up from the steps and hurried to the utility shed. Together, they loaded up Abbie's car with a long, slender pole with a rope loop at one end; two nets; three pairs of heavy gloves; two blankets; two large animal carriers; three safety whistles and a first-aid kit.

Abbie closed the office door behind her. "I've got the directions," she said. "It's just a few minutes away."

The team piled into the car, and headed down the stony driveway past the sign that read, *Wild Paws and Claws Clinic and Rehabilitation Centre.*

Max was quiet. She tried to imagine where two orphaned bear cubs might be hiding. What if they were wandering in the woods, sad and hungry? What if they were hurt? Worst of all, what if Max, Sarah and Abbie couldn't find them?

Chapter Three

Two Perches

"There. I think that's the place," Abbie said, jutting her chin toward a white wood-sided house. It was at the end of a row of houses. The forest began on the other side of it. A small sign in front of the house said, *The Perches*.

"You know, Matthew Perch is at our school," Sarah said to Max in a low voice. "It must have been his dad who killed the mother bear."

Max's eyes widened. She knew who Matthew Perch was. Everyone at school was a bit scared of him. Matthew was in grade six. He was always alone, with his hands jammed in his pockets and a scowl on his face.

"I hope he's not here," Sarah said as Abbie came to a stop.

There was a man standing near the back of the house, holding a hoe. He wore blue overalls and a backwards baseball hat. He watched Abbie, Max and Sarah get out of the car. He didn't move.

Abbie hoisted her backpack over her shoulder and headed toward the man. The girls followed slowly behind. "Hello," Abbie called in a friendly voice. "Mr. Perch?" Still the man didn't move. Abbie walked closer. "Mr. Perch? Are you Mr. Perch?"

The man stared at her. Abbie kept going until she was right in front of him. She thrust out her hand. "I'm Abigail Abernathy. I'm the owner of Wild Paws and Claws."

Finally the man took one hand off the hoe. He shook her hand briefly and grunted, "I'm Perch."

"We heard that there might be two black bear cubs on your property, or nearby. Do we have your permission to look around for them, sir?" Abbie asked. Her voice was light and breezy.

Mr. Perch didn't speak. The question hung in the air, and Max began to get butterflies in her stomach. Maybe he would say no. Then what would they do? How could they leave without looking for the cubs?

Mr. Perch dipped his head once. "Yeah," he grumbled. Then he turned, dropped his hoe by the back door of the house and disappeared inside.

Max breathed a sigh of relief.

"Oh, boy," said Sarah.

"All right, let's get busy," Abbie said in a brisk voice. "First we'll look on Perch's property. I don't think we'll find them here, but we'd better check. All sides of the house, under the shed, under the porch, there in those thick bushes and here in these hedges."

The three of them made a quick search, but with no luck.

"Now we'll fan out. We'll work our way, step by step, into the forest." Abbie pulled three balls of string out of her backpack. "Hopefully, we'll hear the cubs before we get too close to them. Remember, even though they're babies, they have sharp claws and will likely be frightened of us. If you see them, stop and call me," Abbie said firmly.

They moved to the forest edge and were just about to head in when Max saw a boy. He was hurrying out of the forest where it met the road. She recognized Matthew Perch. His black hair was standing up in spikes. His hands were jammed in his pants, as usual. But his head was held high and

– could it be? – he was almost smiling.

Sarah had seen him, too. "It's Matthew Perch," she told Abbie.

Right away, before Max could stop her, Abbie called out, "Young man, you must know these woods well. We need your help. We need to find two lost bear cubs."

As Matthew turned to look at them, his scowl returned. "No," he said abruptly. And then he was gone.

Chapter Four

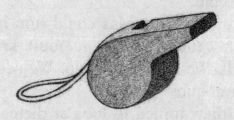

It's Up to Us

"Don't bother with Matthew Perch," Sarah told Abbie, shaking her head. "He probably doesn't care a thing about animals, especially baby ones."

"Is that right?" Abbie asked. "Oh well. We don't have time to persuade him to help us. Let's just do the best we can on our own."

Abbie handed each girl a pair of heavy gloves, a whistle and a ball of string. "Tie one end to a tree here," she instructed. "Unravel it as you go so you can find your way back. Look high and low for the cubs. They might be hard to spot. And don't poke around anywhere with your hands, even with gloves on. You can gently use a stick, if you need to."

Slowly Max began making her way into the woods, in the direction Matthew had come from. As she moved deeper in, she lost sight of Abbie and Sarah.

Max took one step at a time. She didn't want to walk right past the cubs. She looked carefully here and there. Nothing. She stopped and just listened. Nothing. She pushed her stick carefully under bushes and thick underbrush. Still nothing.

How could two cubs be so quiet? How could they hide so well? Were they long gone, deep in the forest?

Max began feeling panicky. Her ball of string was almost all unravelled. When she came to the end, she'd have to stop and turn around.

Then, all of a sudden, something caught her eye. Something up in a tall tree was moving.

Max tiptoed to the base of the tree and peered up through the branches. And then she giggled out loud.

There were two black balls of fur clinging to a high branch. There were two black faces with two brown muzzles and two black noses. Four curious eyes were peering down at her. Max had found the bear cubs!

She quickly blew her whistle for Abbie and

Sarah, and a few minutes later, blew it again.

"Did you find them? Did you find them?" Sarah whispered loudly, making her way through the trees to Max. Abbie was close behind.

Max pointed up to the branch. "Look up there," she said with a smile.

"Oh, two little bear cubs! They're so sweet," Sarah breathed, clasping her hands together in delight. "Just look at their shiny eyes and their little round ears!"

"They are sweet," agreed Abbie. "Good job finding them, Max." Then her voice became serious. "Now, these cubs are scared because they're alone. That's why they've climbed a tree. It's up to us to try to convince them to come down, and that might not be easy. Sarah, can you come with me to get the carriers, the grab pole and the nets? Then we'll see what we can do."

Abbie and Sarah headed back to the Perches', following Max's string. Max was happy to sit on the forest floor, rest against a fallen log and simply watch the cubs. She couldn't take her eyes off them. And the cubs seemed unable to take their eyes off her. They clung to the branch with their sharp claws, not moving. And once in a while they made a soft bleating sound that was so sad, it squeezed

19

Max's heart. *Baa-woww, baa-woww*, they cried.

"Don't worry," she whispered to them soothingly. "I know you're scared without your mother. But it's going to be all right. We'll get you down from there and give you something to fill up your tummies."

But then what? Max wondered. The cubs didn't seem to be injured. But babies couldn't be returned to the wild without their mother. What would happen to them? Could Wild Paws care for two bear cubs? Abbie had managed to look after a bobcat for a whole year. Did she have the skill, and the room, to look after two bears?

Max swallowed hard. First things first. The cubs were up in a tree. The first challenge was to get them down!

When Abbie and Sarah returned, Abbie spoke confidently. "This tree isn't too tall. I'm going to shinny up it until I get near the cubs. I'll try to loop the end of the grab pole around a cub and lower it to the ground. While I do that, I'd like you girls to hold this net directly under the bears. If a cub falls before I can loop it, your job is to catch it in the net! You'll have to hold tight. These fellows look like they each weigh six or seven kilos."

Max and Sarah moved into position. They held

the net at waist level. Max wound the net around her hands to make extra sure she had a good grip.

The cubs could see and hear Abbie coming. They nervously clambered down the branch, toward the end. But as they did, the branch began to bend with their weight. The cub closest to the end stopped and hung on fiercely to keep from falling. But the other cub, closer to Abbie, was as anxious to get as far away from her as possible. It kept moving closer and closer to its sibling even though the branch kept bending with its added weight.

"Uh-oh," warned Max. "Hold on tight, Sarah."

The cub kept inching closer to its sibling, and the branch bent further and further, and all of a sudden, *snap!* The end of it broke off and fell. And with it dropped one unhappy cub.

"Here it comes," sang out Max. Both girls lifted the net a little higher and held on tight, and suddenly, *whompf!* There was a surprised little bear cub in the net, its blue eyes wide and startled. For a moment, the girls didn't move. It had all happened so quickly.

Abbie shinnied down the tree just as fast as she had shinnied up. She reached out with her long arms and scooped the stunned cub from the net. Then, in one quick movement, she loaded it into one of the carriers and latched the door closed. "There's one!" Abbie announced proudly. "Good job, girls!"

Before they could even respond, Abbie was back up the tree. Max and Sarah hurried into position beneath the other cub. The animal looked even more frightened now that it was alone. It sat frozen near the end of the broken branch.

With one arm firmly wrapped around the tree trunk, Abbie reached out for the other cub with the long grab pole.

That's it, Abbie, Max thought. She held her breath as Abbie tried to slip the loop around the scared cub. The forest was so still that Max could hear the cub making whimpering sounds again. And then suddenly, she got a funny feeling. Like someone was watching them.

Max turned and scanned the trees. And then she jumped. She could see a person peeking out from behind a tree. But who was it?

Chapter Five

They Can't Survive

Then Max saw the black spiky hair. It was Matthew Perch.

"Sarah," she whispered. "Sarah, look who's watching us." Max nodded slightly in Matthew's direction.

Sarah's blue eyes widened. "What's he doing here?" she asked in a low voice.

Max shrugged. She looked nervously at Matthew and noticed that he was quite near the first cub's carrier. "He wouldn't try to hurt the bear, would he?"

Sarah frowned. "I don't know. I don't trust him, though," she said.

"Girls, concentrate," Abbie softly scolded.

Max watched as Abbie began inching the loop closer to the baby animal. The frightened cub loosened its tight grip on the branch. It lifted one paw and batted at the rope. That was just what Abbie had been waiting for. She quickly slipped the loop over the cub's head and body, and with a gentle tug, tightened it.

Using all her strength, Abbie climbed partway down the tree, the pole in one hand. The cub dangled helplessly at the end of it and tried to grab at the tree trunk with its claws. But Abbie managed to keep it from clinging on.

As soon as she was close enough, Abbie called, "Here she comes, girls." Abbie carefully dropped the cub end of the pole. The bear fell the short distance and landed directly on the net.

Whompf!

Max couldn't help smiling. This smaller cub looked as surprised and wide-eyed as the first!

In a moment, Abbie was down from the tree and placing the cub inside the second carrier. It was only then that Max looked back to where Matthew had been hiding. The boy had left as quietly as he had come.

"We did it!" cried Sarah. "We have them both."

Abbie breathed heavily. She had worked hard to rescue the cubs. "You girls were terrific with the net," she said. "But our job isn't finished yet. We have to get our equipment and these bear cubs to the car, and head back to Wild Paws. I don't think these guys have had anything to eat for several days – not since their mother was killed. We need to get some nourishment into them as soon as possible."

Max and Sarah knew she was right. They quickly packed their gear into Abbie's backpack. Max and Sarah each took one end of a carrier, heavy with the cub inside. Max carried the grab pole, and Sarah wore the backpack. Abbie hoisted up the other carrier.

Max took another quick look around before they all headed out. Where was Matthew? Why had he come back into the woods to spy on them? His father had shot the mother bear. Was Matthew trying to harm the cubs? Max wasn't sure. The boy looked mean and nasty, but he hadn't actually done anything bad. She didn't know what to think about him.

She put him out of her mind, and eagerly turned her attention to the two little bear cubs that needed her.

Chapter Six

A Friend

The drive back to Wild Paws was quick. But Max and Sarah still had time to get a good look at the cubs and ask Abbie lots of questions.

Max rested her chin on the seat back and gazed at the cubs, first one and then the other. Abbie had placed the carriers side by side in the back so the cubs wouldn't feel lonely.

"The cubs look almost exactly the same," Max remarked. "But not quite. They both have really cute round ears, small tails and small blue eyes. But this one is bigger." She pointed to the cub on the left. It was sitting on its hind legs, just like a dog. It seemed nervous. It poked its nose against the side of the car-

rier and touched the other cub's fur. It seemed to be making sure that its sibling was still there.

"And he has a little white patch of fur on his chest," Max noted. Suddenly she had a wonderful idea. "I just thought of a name for him," she cried. "Let's call him Patch!"

Sarah nodded. "I like that." She was looking at the cubs thoughtfully. "You know, the cubs are so small now. It's hard to imagine that one day they'll be huge."

"Yes, perhaps ten, twenty, or even thirty times the weight they are now," Abbie said. She was driving very slowly. She was always a cautious driver, but when she had animals in the car, Max noticed, she took extra care.

"What do black bears eat?" Max asked Abbie. "They must need a lot of food!"

"They do," agreed Abbie. "Black bears are omnivorous, which means that they eat many kinds of food, such as insects, small mammals and even fish. But they mostly eat plants and fruit. They especially like berries – tiny berries! A big black bear has to eat a lot of berries to fill up. It picks them off bushes with its lips and long tongue. Sometimes a bear will find a large berry patch . . ."

"There's another good reason for naming this cub Patch!" Sarah whispered to Max.

". . . and it will eat and eat and eat that one species of berry for days or even weeks, until they're all gone! Only then will it move off in search of other food."

Abbie turned down Hare Bell Lane. They were close to home now.

"Do bears eat all kinds of berries?" Max asked.

"Raspberries, blackberries, elderberries, strawberries . . . whatever types grow where they live," she told Max.

Max looked at the smaller bear cub and grinned. "I have an idea for this cub's name," she said, nudging Sarah with her elbow. "She's a black bear, right? And she'll eat blackberries when she grows up, right? So why don't we call her . . . "

"Blackberry!" Sarah chimed in. "And she's round and roly-poly — just like a berry!"

Abbie turned down the stony driveway that led to the rehabilitation centre. It was almost dinnertime now. Max's stomach grumbled. It reminded her that the cubs hadn't eaten in several days.

"Abbie, what will we feed the cubs?" Max asked in a tight voice. "They must be starving!"

Abbie didn't speak for a minute. She parked the car and turned to look at Max. "We'll do our best to find something. We didn't know what to feed Tuffy at first, but it all worked out."

"OK," Max answered, feeling reassured.

They all got out of the car, and Abbie opened the trunk. "I think we should carry the cubs into one of the examining rooms," she said thoughtfully. "That might be the best place for them until we can – "

But then a voice interrupted. "Isn't anyone going to say hello to an old friend?"

Max, Sarah and Abbie turned. "Randall!" they cried when they saw the young man heading toward them. The girls rushed over to greet him.

"Randall, what are you doing here?" cried Max. "How did you know we needed a vet right now?"

"Are you done university? Are you visiting your aunt, Mrs. Peach?" asked Sarah.

"Whoa! That's a lot of questions," said Randall, shaking his head. He was wearing khaki pants and a red shirt that was half tucked in. He scratched at his ear nervously. "Yes, I'm visiting my aunt. Yes, I have finished school for the year. And I didn't know you needed a vet. I just happened to drop by today to see how you all were." He pushed his shaggy hair out of his eyes.

"Well, Randall," said Abbie, striding up. "You always seem to arrive when there is some excitement going on at Wild Paws. But we're happy to see you. And Max is right, we could use a vet now."

Randall scratched his ear again, considering. "It's nice to see you, too, Abbie. But remember, I've only finished my second year of veterinary school. I haven't had much experience with wild animals yet. I'm not sure if . . . "

Max tugged at Randall's arm. "Come on, Randall. We need your help."

"Please?" begged Sarah.

"We've just rescued two orphaned bear cubs from a tree," explained Max. "Come and have a look." She led him to the back of the car. "Here are Patch and Blackberry."

One of the two black balls of fur moved. Patch scratched at his ear with his large paw and yawned. His tongue and the inside of his mouth were a soft pink. Blackberry remained still. Her small eyes gazed steadily at Max.

"The cubs' mother was killed several days ago. They haven't eaten since," Abbie told Randall. "They look healthy, but if you could just check them over and reassure us, we'd appreciate it."

Max still clung to Randall's arm. She remembered how he had helped an injured mother snowshoe hare that spring. Randall had been uncertain about helping then, too. He had once made a mistake when treating an injured squirrel, and lost confidence in himself as a vet. But in the end, he had done his best and saved the hare.

"Randall, take a look at Patch," Max said. "Can

you see how we chose his name? Look at the nice white patch of fur on his belly."

Randall looked closely at the sleepy bear cub. "I see it," he grinned.

Patch lifted his other paw and rubbed at his eyes. "He looks just like a tired toddler," giggled Sarah.

Patch yawned once more and curled back up into a furry ball. He lay as close to Blackberry as he could. Blackberry shifted a little, then poked her nose at Patch through the side of the carrier.

"Look at Blackberry," Max said. "She likes to stick close to her brother. But Patch probably didn't like it much when they were up in the tree. Blackberry kept edging nearer to him on the branch. Patch was on the end that finally broke."

Randall smiled. "I can just picture it!" he said. "OK, I'll give the cubs a check-up. I think I've learned enough to be able to do a good job at that."

Sarah gave Max an excited thumbs-up, and Max breathed a sigh of relief.

"While I do that, you should probably get them something to eat. I guess you don't have any bear milk on hand, do you, Abbie?" he asked, a twinkle in his eye.

Abbie cocked her head to one side and grinned at him. "No. All out." Then the look on her face became serious. "What would be the best thing for these fellows? They must be extremely hungry."

Randall thought for a moment.

But suddenly, Max had an idea. "What did you first feed Tuffy when I brought her here?" she asked Abbie.

Abbie took off her glasses and tried to remember. "I fed her goat's milk from a small baby bottle. It was all I had. Then you found the bobcat expert and she helped us create a special formula that was similar to a mother bobcat's milk."

"Goat's milk," repeated Randall. "That might work for now. Just to get something into them."

"And then we can find out what to feed the bear cubs permanently," Max piped in.

Abbie put her hand on Max's shoulder. "Max, it would be wonderful if you and Sarah did some research. But there's something you should know." Max looked up at Abbie's worried face. "We won't be able to keep these cubs here until they are ready to return to the wild. We were able to look after Tuffy because she wasn't too big. We had enough space for her. And with all your fundraising, we've been able to supply her with food — even now that she's almost grown and eating so much.

"But Wild Paws and Claws just doesn't have the funds to care for two growing bear cubs. Or the space. We can't keep them here, and we can't return these baby bear cubs to the wild — not without their mother — not yet. We need to find Patch and Blackberry another place where they can be cared for until they are ready to be returned to the wild. And we need to find that special place soon."

Chapter Seven

Hungry Cubs

"Can you give me a hand, Max and Sarah?" Randall asked.

Max wanted to shake off the anxious feeling that Abbie's words had given her. Instead of worrying about an animal, she knew that the best thing was to do something for it. She always felt better to be helping.

So she cheerfully took one end of Patch's carrier, and she and Sarah lifted it out of the back of the car. Randall reached in to get Blackberry's carrier.

"Don't worry, Patch," Max told the little bear kindly. "This might feel like a swinging branch, but we're not going to let you drop this time!"

As gently as they could, the girls set Patch's carrier down on the floor of the examining room. Randall set Blackberry's right next to it, so the cubs could continue to stay close to each other. "While you examine the cubs, we'll see if Abbie needs help," Max told Randall.

Abbie was checking containers in the small fridge. "Well, we don't seem to have any goat's milk on hand," said Abbie. Suddenly she snapped her fingers. "I know!"

She began rummaging through cupboards. "Girls, give me a hand, please. I'm looking for a box with a picture of a dog on it. You know how some babies — humans, that is — drink formula? You add the powdered mix to boiling water. Well, animals can't drink formula made for humans. It hurts their tummies. But there is a special formula made for puppies. It's a synthetic dog's milk substitute. I think I have some here, and it might be just the thing to whip up for our hungry cubs."

The girls joined in the search. A few minutes later Max asked, "Is this it?" She handed a box to Abbie.

"You bet. Good work," Abbie said, climbing down from her chair. "Now, I'll put the kettle on, and perhaps you could look for some bottles,

Sarah. Try in these lower cupboards."

Sarah eagerly did as she was asked.

"You know, we haven't used them since we bottle-fed Tuffy," Abbie recalled. "Which reminds me. We were supposed to have a chat about her today, before all the excitement with the cubs got us sidetracked!"

Again Max felt the funny combination of butterflies in her stomach and joy in her heart.

"We've done a good job of raising her," Abbie said.

"And this is a good time of year for her to be released," Sarah added. She stood up and closed the cupboard doors. She had a bottle in each hand. "It's almost summer."

"Yes," Abbie said. "We just need a vet to examine her now. If she's healthy, I think it's time for her to be set free."

Max nodded, but she couldn't speak. The kettle whistled and Max unplugged it.

"We should ask Randall to look at her," Abbie went on. "If he will, and she's healthy, we should release her in the next day or two."

In the next day or two? Still Max couldn't speak. How could she say goodbye to Tuffy? She had been taking care of the bobcat for a whole year. How could she possibly give her up so soon?

As Abbie and Sarah mixed the formula, Max answered her own question: Because I care about her. And because Tuffy isn't mine. She doesn't belong to anyone. She belongs to the wilderness. She needs to be free.

Max swallowed, and then spoke firmly. "Good idea. Maybe Randall will even do it now, this evening."

Abbie smiled at Max with understanding eyes. "Some things about this job just aren't easy, are they girls?" She glanced at the formula. "Now, could you each pour some into the bottles, please? Make sure it's just warm and not too hot."

The girls did as she instructed, and then placed a rubber nipple on top of each bottle.

"Right. Let's go," said Abbie.

* * *

"Well, good news," Randall said cheerily. He was taking off a pair of surgical gloves. "I've just finished having a good look at these two cubs, and they're both in fine health. A little hungry, maybe, but not injured in any way."

"Oh, good," breathed Max.

"Randall, we have something else to ask of you," Abbie said. "We wondered if you would have a quick look at Tuffy while you're here. We think she's in good health, but we need a vet's approval before we can release her. If you'll do that for us, we can set her free very soon."

Randall hesitated, but then he caught himself. "Of course I will," he said. "I appreciate your trust in me."

"Randall, you're good at what you do. It's that simple," Abbie said. "And we need you! If you want to head over to Tuffy's enclosure, I'll get the girls started on feeding Patch and Blackberry."

Max's and Sarah's mouths dropped open. They looked at one another and then at Abbie. Was she really going to let them feed the bear cubs?

Chapter Eight

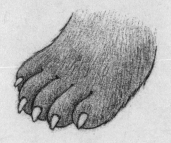

A Drop of Milk

Abbie put on a thick pair of work gloves. She opened Patch's carrier door and lifted him out. "Come on, girls," she said. "Put on a pair of gloves and a work shirt, and let's get busy! Who wants to feed Patch?"

Max and Sarah couldn't believe their good fortune. "Um, I will," stammered Max eagerly.

Sarah added, "I'll feed Blackberry."

"OK, come on, Max. Sit right over here. It won't be much different from feeding Tuffy in the early days, except that this cub is a little bigger. Remember, watch out for his claws. They are very sharp. Patch could hurt you without meaning to.

Hold him firmly, but not tight. Keep your face away."

Max put on an old work shirt and thick gloves. She sat down and reached out her arms, and Abbie handed Patch to her.

Max couldn't believe it. She had a bear cub in her lap!

Patch was heavy, about the weight of a small dog. He immediately began to squirm. He turned toward Max and started to climb up her arm. Max was glad to be wearing two shirt layers as she felt his claws dig into her.

She got a firmer hold on the bear. Then she took the warm bottle and put it in his mouth. Would Patch drink? Would he like the formula?

Immediately the cub began sucking. Max breathed a sigh of relief. With every swallow, Patch was getting nutrition. He was building up strength.

Soon Patch loosened his grip on Max's arm and relaxed into her lap. Max watched his eyes slowly close as he drank. She gently touched the white fur on his chest. She felt the warmth of the cub against her belly. She saw his ears twitch once or twice. She admired the tip of his black nose. He drank and he drank and then the bottle was empty. Patch lay still. He was sound asleep.

Only then did Max look over at Sarah. Blackberry was just finishing her bottle. After a final noisy slurp, she heaved a big sigh. Then she gave a loud burp. The girls giggled. With one more sigh, Blackberry, too, fell asleep.

Max and Sarah sat quietly with the content baby bears in their laps. Max wished the moment would never end.

Patch's paws were still wrapped around the bottle. A drop of milk clung to his lip. She watched the sides of his full belly move slowly in and out as he slept. The cubs were no longer alone. They were no longer frightened and hungry. They were in a safe place where people would care for them.

But for how long?

Max looked down at Patch. How cute he was, from the tops of his round ears to the tip of his short tail! Soon he would grow into a large black bear. That is, if she and Sarah and Abbie could find the cubs a safe place to stay. Could they do it?

Max touched Patch lightly with the tip of her gloved finger. His mother was gone. He was depending on them. So was Blackberry.

Max took a deep breath. "Don't worry," she

promised the little cub. "We'll look after you. We'll find you a new home."

Chapter Nine

Farewell

It was Saturday morning. As Max and her younger brother David gulped down breakfast, their father came downstairs in his pyjamas. "Why are you up so early, kids?" Mr. Kearney yawned. He rubbed his eyes and wandered to the table.

"We need to get to Wild Paws right away, Dad," Max said between bites of toast. "Remember I told you last night? We're letting Tuffy go today. Randall checked her over last night, and she's very healthy. We're releasing her back into the forest first thing this morning."

"Oh, yes," Max's father said. "I must still be half asleep to have forgotten that." He sat down at the table. "That's very exciting."

Max's grandmother appeared in the doorway of the kitchen. "It seems like just the other day that the kids and I found that tiny little kitten," she said.

"At first we thought she was a baby cat. Remember, Max?" David said, gulping down his orange juice.

Mrs. Kearney came in from the kitchen, wiping her hands on a dishtowel. She saw the expression on Max's face. "Well, it's wonderful that Tuffy will be free again. But it will be sad for you to say goodbye."

"Yeah," Max agreed. "I really love her. And I'll miss her."

Mrs. Kearney hugged Max. "I'm proud of you," she told her quietly. "Good luck."

"Thanks, Mom," said Max. "Oh, and don't expect me back until the end of the day. Abbie will probably need some extra help feeding and watering the animals today, and maybe we'll get to feed Patch and Blackberry again, too. Plus, Sarah and I have to do some research. We need to find out if there's a bear rehab centre near us. We have to find a new home for Patch and Blackberry."

Mrs. Kearney smiled. "OK. Then I guess we'll

see David and Grandma around lunchtime and you at dinner."

Max and David jumped into Grandma's car. They picked up Sarah and in a short time were heading up the driveway to Wild Paws and Claws.

In the morning sunshine, they could see Randall standing by Abbie's station wagon. He waved at the girls.

"Randall, you're here!" Max exclaimed in delight, hurrying over.

The young man put a finger to his lips, urging her to be quiet. "I wanted to make sure that Tuffy got away all right." He pointed into the back of the car.

Max looked in. There was a large carrier covered with a heavy tarpaulin. She knew that Tuffy was inside. She wanted to lift the covering and look at the bobcat. She wanted to see her tufted ears, her ruffed cheeks and her alert orange eyes. She wanted to admire the tawny brown coat covered with black spots. But she knew that it was best not to disturb Tuffy. They had worked so hard to keep the bobcat wild. Tuffy had never learned to accept humans. This was what would help her now to survive on her own.

"Good morning, all," Abbie said briskly. "It looks

like Tuffy is ready." The tall woman glanced at each of them in turn. "And we're ready. So let's go. Max and Sarah, you can drive with me. Randall, perhaps you could drive with David and his grandmother. I'll be the lead car. Just follow along."

As she climbed into the car, Max asked, "Abbie, how are the cubs? Are they still OK?"

Abbie's face blossomed into a smile. "They're great," she said. "We'll feed them again when we get back."

The trip took about two hours. To Max, it went by in a flash. Even though she couldn't see the bobcat, she could hear her move in the carrier once in a while. She was happy just to be near Tuffy. Max spent the entire ride thinking about her year with Tuffy – from the first time she had seen her tiny face until today, the day she would go home.

Finally, Abbie headed down a stony side road. The car bumped and bounced. Max and Sarah reached back to steady the carrier.

Abbie and Grandma parked their cars at the end of a grassy lane, by a small wood.

"Where are we?" asked David. "It's like we're in the middle of nowhere!"

"Exactly," said Abbie, grinning. "We are in the middle of nowhere. This is Tuffy's new home turf!"

Abbie and Randall opened the back of the car and lifted out the carrier. Then Abbie adjusted her round glasses. She cleared her throat. "I'm sure you would all like to say goodbye to Tuffy. Why don't you come and have a moment with her, one by one?"

Sarah went first, then David and then Grandma. They each crouched down and took one final look at the beautiful bobcat through an opening in the tarpaulin. Abbie had given Grandma permission to take one last photo of her. It would be kept with all the other pictures that celebrated Tuffy's life at the clinic, from rescue to release.

"Max, I wonder if you would come with Randall and me," Abbie said gently. She looked over the top of her glasses at Max.

Max couldn't speak. She gave one quick nod. Abbie and Randall picked up the carrier and headed into the trees, and Max followed.

When they were out of sight of the road, Abbie tilted her head toward a flat area beneath a grove of trees. She and Randall set the carrier down there. Max breathed in the warm fresh air. The breeze brushed the long grasses that bordered the grove. In the distance, a flock of birds suddenly rose into the air. Below them, sunlight sparkled on a stretch of river. Beyond the meadow were rocky outcroppings, and more trees as far as Max could see. This looked like a perfect place for Tuffy to live.

As Abbie and Randall pulled the tarpaulin completely away, Max saw Tuffy, and felt a burst of happiness. The bobcat stood up. Her ears flicked this way and that. She sniffed again and again. This was her new world!

Abbie handed Max her gloves, and motioned for her to put them on. She spoke softly, "Once, you rescued Tuffy. Now you should be the one to release her."

Max squeezed Abbie's hand in thanks. It was a wonderful honour.

She moved next to the cage. "How beautiful you are." Max barely breathed the words. But as she did so, Tuffy looked up at her.

Max stared back. For a moment, there was a stillness in the bobcat's eyes. Max didn't dare blink. She held the bobcat's steady gaze. I'll never forget you, Max said, this time silently.

Then Tuffy's eyes widened and she startled. She moved away from Max, and crouched down against the side of the cage, frightened. Her ears were flattened back against her skull.

Max sighed. This was as it should be. It was a

good thing that Tuffy was afraid of humans, and even afraid of her.

Max knew that the bobcat couldn't wait any longer. "Goodbye, Tuffy. Good luck." Max reached down and opened the latch of the carrier. She swung the door open wide, then swiftly moved back to stand with Abbie and Randall.

Tuffy didn't move at first. Then, in one graceful movement, she sprang forward out of the carrier. Her paws touched the ground. There was no enclosure to hold her in. She was free.

With a flick of her bobtail, she leaped between the trees. The bobcat seemed to melt away into the waving meadow grasses. Tuffy was gone.

Chapter Ten

A Loud Bang

"Max?" Sarah leaned across the back seat of the car. She shook her friend's arm gently. "Open your eyes, Max. We're back at Wild Paws. We've got work to do."

Max sighed. She didn't move. "Sarah, I feel so strange. I feel like I'm floating on a cloud because Tuffy is free." She sighed again. "But on the other hand, I'm so sad because she's gone."

Sarah nodded. "I feel a bit that way too. Like sweet and sour sauce."

Max giggled. "Oh, Sarah. That's just it! Like sweet and sour sauce!"

Laughing with Sarah made Max feel much better.

Maybe it was OK to taste a little sadness and a little happiness at the same time. Maybe she could get used to it.

Abbie called to the girls from the front steps of the clinic. "We'll feed the cubs now. Then I have to make a few phone calls. I need to order some more food for the raccoons and Tippy."

"OK," Max and Sarah called back. "We're coming." The girls headed eagerly across the parking lot to the clinic. But they had only gone a few steps when Max stopped.

"Just a minute, Sarah," she warned. Her eyes were fixed on the stand of trees that separated the office building from the animal pens.

"What is it?" Sarah asked. "What's wrong?" She anxiously twirled the end of one of her braids.

"I think I saw someone. There. In those trees," said Max.

"Oh, it's probably just Randall," Sarah said. But then the girls saw Randall. He was in the utility shed putting away Tuffy's carrier. As the young vet closed the door to the shed, he waved goodbye to the girls and headed down the driveway.

If it wasn't Randall, who was it?

Max and Sarah looked at one another. At the same time they said, "Matthew Perch."

Max looked back toward the trees. "Now I can't see anyone there. Did you see him?" she asked.

"No," said Sarah, shaking her head. "I didn't." She thought for a moment. "Maybe he wasn't actually there. Maybe you just imagined you saw someone."

"Maybe," Max said. It was what she wanted to believe. What would Matthew Perch be doing here, anyway?

"Then let's forget it," Sarah said. She took Max's arm. "Come on, let's go and feed the cubs."

"OK," Max said uncertainly. She glanced once more toward the trees. Nothing.

* * *

Max, Sarah and Abbie entered the room where the bear cubs waited in their carriers. Patch and Blackberry were trying to play together. Blackberry's claws poked through the slits in the carrier. Her head was pressed against the side, and Patch was trying to gnaw on her ear.

"I think we'll put the cubs in Tuffy's old outdoor enclosure after I'm done with my phone calls," Abbie told the girls. "They can't spend much more time cooped up in these small carriers. They can stay out there until . . . " Abbie stopped. She frowned and rubbed her forehead.

"Until we find them a new home nearby," Max said cheerfully, finishing her sentence for her. "Sarah and I are going to get right to work on that after we've fed them."

"Good," Abbie said. "It's great that I can always count on you two to help."

Max and Sarah quickly got comfortable on the floor. Each girl held a bottle of warm formula. Abbie took Patch out of his carrier.

"Do you want to switch cubs this time?" Abbie asked. "Sarah, do you want to feed Patch?"

"Well," Sarah said, glancing at Max. "If it's OK with Max, I'd prefer to feed Blackberry again."

Max smiled. It was no wonder that Sarah was her best friend. "Of course it's OK. I was actually hoping to feed Patch again," she replied.

The bear cubs finished their bottles all too soon. Again, they dozed off to sleep once their stomachs were full. Reluctantly, Max lifted the sleeping Patch into Abbie's arms. Soon the cubs were back in their carriers.

As the girls put away their work clothes, they heard Abbie close the clinic door. They heard the door close again as they entered the small kitchen. "I guess it didn't shut properly the first time," Max said.

As Max washed the cubs' bottles and Sarah tidied up, Max wondered if she'd have another chance to feed Patch later that day. She loved holding him. She loved seeing him close up.

Then suddenly, from the clinic, came a loud bang. Both girls froze. They stared at each other.

What could it be?

Chapter Eleven

Is Patch Hurt?

Max ran to the door and looked down the hallway. She caught her breath.

It was Matthew Perch. He held Blackberry's carrier in one hand. Patch's carrier sat by his feet. The broken handle was still in his hand.

"What are you doing?" Max cried. "Is Patch hurt?" She ran down the hallway and crouched by the cub's carrier. He was awake and staring up at her, trembling. But otherwise he looked unharmed.

"You could have hurt him!" Max howled, her hands on her hips. Her eyes flashed angrily. "Or maybe that's exactly what you were trying to do!"

"No, no," Matthew replied. His face was red. He looked flustered.

"Well, then what *were* you trying to do?" It was Sarah, standing in the doorway. "Where did you think you were taking these bear cubs?"

"Hey," said the boy. He hadn't let go of Blackberry's carrier. "Bear cubs belong in the forest. You're the ones who took them away from their home, not me." He narrowed his eyes. "I'm just trying to put them back where they belong."

"You're trying to take the cubs back to the forest?" Sarah asked in disbelief.

Matthew nodded. "Yes, I am," he said. His face went red again. "I'm trying to protect them."

Max and Sarah stared at the boy.

"I know my dad killed their mother," he said. His gaze fell to the floor. "I feel awful about that. But that's no reason to bring them here and throw them in a cage and keep them locked up forever. They belong in the forest."

Matthew tossed away the broken handle and reached down to pick up Patch's carrier with his free arm.

"Wait, wait, Matthew," said Max, holding up her hand. "I think you've got it wrong. We know the cubs belong in the forest," she said. "We want them to be there, too. But these baby bears can't survive on their own."

Matthew still struggled to lift the carrier, but he was listening. "Why not?" he said coldly.

"Cubs still need their mother's milk to survive. They need to be taught how and what to eat. They'd die, alone in the forest. All we wanted to do was capture them, feed them and find a way to return them to the woods." Max looked Matthew in the eye. "I think that's what you want too, isn't it?"

Matthew stood up. "Well, yeah," he stammered. "I–I just wanted – "

"Now, unfortunately they can't stay at Wild Paws for much longer. Abbie says we need to find a bear rehab centre near here that can care for them. Sarah and I were just going to see if we could find a place like that." Max paused. "Maybe you could help us. That is, if you really want to help the cubs."

Max held her breath. She couldn't believe that she'd actually invited Matthew to help them. She couldn't believe that she was starting to think he might not be so bad after all. Matthew leaned down and picked up Patch's carrier. Max stood firm. There was no way that he was going to walk away with those cubs. But instead of trying to push past her, Matthew turned and put the carriers gently back on the examining-room floor.

"OK," he said. "I'll help."

Chapter Twelve

Bears Are Wild

Abbie was still on the phone when Max, Sarah and Matthew came into the office. She raised her eyebrows when she saw the boy, and then gave him a quick welcoming smile.

Sarah and Max logged onto the Internet.

"Look at this," Max cried. "These cubs are just about the same size as Patch and Blackberry! Read the caption: *Sibling bear cubs share a strong bond. They need to stay together in the wild for protection, especially when their mother isn't around. Playing together helps them form the strong relationship that can keep them safe.*"

"This is interesting, too," Sarah said. "*When bears*

leave their dens in spring, food is scarce. Then green plants begin to grow. Bears begin to eat young leaves and grass. Cubs begin to taste what their mother eats, but they still depend on her milk."

"I could read about bears all day. But we really should be checking out bear rehab centres," said Max.

"Try searching for 'black bear rehabilitation,'" said Matthew. Max glanced up at the boy, surprised to hear him speak up.

Sarah typed in the words. Right away, several choices appeared. One was for a Canadian centre called Bears Are Wild.

"Oh, look!" Max exclaimed. "Try that one, Sarah."

The computer screen filled with a beautiful colour photo of three young bear cubs in a large enclosure. One cub sat on the branch of a tall pine tree. Another splashed in a small natural pond. The third lay on a large flat rock. There was a log climbing structure, and logs were scattered about.

"Bears Are Wild is run by a woman named Madeleine Brant," Max said. "This is what she says: *I accept orphaned bear cubs. But this is not a zoo. I raise the cubs so that they can be returned to the wild.*

Call me for information or help. She lists her e-mail address and phone number."

"And look," said Sarah. "Here's the address. Bears Are Wild is near the town of Bridgehurst."

"Bridgehurst isn't too far from here," Matthew told them. "About two hours by car."

Max clasped her hands together. "This could be just the place for Patch and Blackberry!"

Just then Abbie put down the phone. "What's that?" she asked.

"Abbie, Abbie!" Sarah cried. "Come and look! We think we've found a rehab centre for Patch and Blackberry."

Abbie stood up and peered through her glasses at Matthew. "And *whooo* are you?" she asked kindly. "I think I've seen you before."

"Matthew Perch, ma'am," said the boy. He looked at Max and Sarah. They could have told Abbie that he had tried to steal Patch and Blackberry. But the girls said nothing. A look of relief crept over Matthew's face.

"Nice to meet you. Glad to have you helping out," Abbie said. "Now, what have we here?" She looked at the web page for Bears Are Wild. "Well, this certainly looks like a fine place for our two cubs. I'll call right now and find out a little more.

Good work, girls . . . and boy." She smiled.

Ten minutes later, Abbie hung up the phone. "Madeleine would be pleased to have two new cubs to care for. She'd like us to bring them as soon as possible." Abbie thought for a moment. "Today is Saturday. We can't wait until next weekend. But you have school during the week . . . "

Max held her breath. She wanted to see Bears Are Wild. She wanted to see Patch and Blackberry introduced to their new home.

"Well, there's only one thing for it. We'll simply have to go tomorrow."

"Thanks, Abbie!" cried Max. She and Sarah gave each other a quick hug. "We'll ask our parents. But I'm sure it'll be fine with them."

Then Max noticed Matthew. He was standing awkwardly in the corner. His hands were jammed deep in his pockets. "Abbie, what about Matthew?" she said. "Can he come too?"

Abbie looked surprised. "Well, of course Matthew can come. I just assumed that we'd all go. If you'd like to, that is, Matthew."

Matthew didn't look up, but he nodded.

Max liked Matthew more now than she had before. But . . . she was still uncertain about him. The feeling was sort of sweet and sour, all mixed around inside her. It was easier before, when she didn't have to think about liking him at all.

Chapter Thirteen

Bear Woman

Sunday morning was bright and sunny. Max was waiting by the front door when Abbie's station wagon pulled up.

"Hi, Abbie," said Max as she climbed in. She looked over the back seat. The two cubs were curled up in their carriers. "Hello, Patch and Blackberry," she greeted them.

They picked up Sarah next, and then Matthew. Then they set off for Bears Are Wild.

Max rolled down the car window and felt the warm breeze on her face. Every few minutes she turned and checked on the cubs. Abbie hadn't put them in the outdoor pen yesterday, and this morning, they couldn't settle down. They kept getting up and stretching, and trying to play with each other through the carrier walls.

"Don't worry. Soon you'll be out of there and you can have a real play together!" Max whispered.

Once they reached Bridgehurst, Sarah began reading out directions. It was after noon when Max called out, "There it is! I see a sign!"

Abbie pulled into a long driveway lined with trees. She parked beside a small farmhouse with a wide veranda. Max, Sarah and Matthew climbed out of the car and stretched. A small border collie came running up to them. The screen door opened and a young woman came out. She wore brown shorts, a khaki shirt, rolled-up socks and hiking boots. Her long hair was clipped back on both sides.

She held out her hand. "I'm Madeleine Brant. They call me Bear Woman around here. Happy to meet you all."

In a moment the carriers were out of the car and Madeleine was exclaiming in delight over Patch and Blackberry. "They look quite healthy!" she said with a pleased smile. "Their mother was taking good care of them. And you've done a good job getting some food into them after their days alone."

Max just had to ask the Bear Woman a question. "We rehabilitated a bobcat named Tuffy," she told her. "But we wore special costumes so Tuffy wouldn't know humans were caring for her. We disguised our smell and we never spoke near her. Is that what you do here with the bears?"

Madeleine looked impressed. "What an interesting idea. No, I don't wear a costume. I don't disguise my smell, and I talk to the bears sometimes." She paused. "Different wildlife workers have different ways of looking after animals and trying to return them to the wild." She looked seriously at Max. "One thing I've learned from the bears here at Bears Are Wild is that they are smart! I believe that they can tell people apart. The bears get to know me as I feed them and teach them things. They recognize me, and they trust me. But they remain very nervous of other people."

Max smiled. She could tell that Patch and Blackberry would be in good hands.

Madeleine grinned. "So, let's take the cubs to see their new home!"

They all followed Madeleine as she led them behind the house and down a trail into the woods. It was quiet and peaceful. Birds fluttered through the trees, and sunlight dappled the path.

They emerged into a small clearing, and there, in an enclosure, were the three bears from the web page. Two of them wrestled playfully near the pond. One lay atop the climbing structure.

"These are Bruno and Charcoal," said Madeleine, pointing to the scuffling cubs. "And this one is Butterball. They were all tiny when they arrived here last year. Butterball was taken from her den by a hiker at only two months old. Bruno was caught in an illegal snare trap, and Charcoal was orphaned when a car hit his mother. I became their mother. I had to bottle-feed them all. I cared for them and taught them the things a mother bear would have taught them. And they taught me lots of things, too!"

Matthew stood beside Abbie. Max noticed that there wasn't the trace of a scowl on his face. In fact, his eyes looked lit up from inside. He had looked like that the other day, coming out of the forest. Suddenly Max understood. He must have gone looking for the bear cubs after their mother was killed. When he saw them on the tree branch, he thought they were safe. That must be why he had looked so happy.

Matthew spoke up. "When do you return them to the wild?"

"Good question," Madeleine said. "Some cubs, such as these three, are still small in the fall. They aren't ready to be released. They spend the winter in the den that I've built inside the enclosure. Come and see."

They followed Madeleine around the outside of the enclosure. At the very back, through the mesh, she pointed out a large wooden box with a square doorway, set in among several low trees and bushes. "When winter really sets in, the bears settle in here and don't come out until springtime!"

As the group walked back to the front of the enclosure, Madeleine went on, "If the cubs are healthy and full-size in the fall, like these three are now, I take them into the woods at the end of the year. I put a radio collar on them so that our local scientists can track them and learn more about black bears. Then I tranquilize them and place them in one of the natural bear dens that I know about. Or I put them in one of the artificial dens that I have prepared in the summer. When they wake up, they might come out and wander around a bit. Then they go back to that den and sleep away the winter, or find another den for their winter snooze."

"And what about Patch and Blackberry?" asked Matthew.

"I'm not sure yet," Madeleine told him. "I think we'll wait and see how they do. They might need to spend a winter here with me, or perhaps I'll be able to release them with the other three this year." Madeleine spread her arms. "I'll do my best to make the right decision for them," she promised.

Then she clasped her hands together. "And now, what do you think? Should we put the bears in their new home? Do you want them to live here with me until they're ready to be set free?" Madeleine looked seriously at each of the girls, at Matthew and, lastly, at Abbie.

No one had to think twice. "Yes," was the unanimous response.

Madeleine scooped up Blackberry's carrier. Then she asked, "Who will help me bring Patch into the enclosure?"

Sarah shook her head. "Not me, thanks. I'll watch from out here."

Max looked at Patch. She looked at his cute black nose and the little splash of white fur on his chest. Then she looked at Matthew. He was staring at the ground.

"I think Matthew would like to," Max suggested.

Matthew's head snapped up and his eyes turned

to her, amazed. Then he turned to Madeleine. "Yeah," he agreed. "I would like to." His eyes swung back to Max and he smiled.

It only took a moment. Madeleine opened Blackberry's carrier first. Blackberry didn't budge, so Madeleine tipped up the carrier slightly. Blackberry scrambled to keep her footing, then slid ungracefully out the door and landed on her bottom.

With a surprised *baa-woww, baa-woww*, Blackberry scurried away. She headed for the nearest tree and was up the trunk in the blink of an eye. She climbed to the first branch and then stopped.

Next Matthew unlatched Patch's carrier. The little black cub had seen his sister head for the tree. Without hesitating, he tumbled out of the carrier and didn't pause until he was sitting side by side, on the branch, with Blackberry.

Max couldn't help giggling. "That's exactly the way they were when we first saw them," she said. "Two cute little cubs, hiding up in a tree."

"Except the cubs are safe and sound now," Sarah added. "Now they're here!"

Madeleine grinned. "And they can stay up there as long as they want. But you can bet that as soon as I come in here with a few bottles of formula,

they'll be down out of that tree in a flash."

Max smiled. "Can we come back and visit them sometimes? Just look at them from out here, I mean?" she asked.

"Please do," Madeleine encouraged.

As they drove away from Bears Are Wild, Max was thoughtful. She looked over at Matthew. She still had a sweet-and-sour feeling about him. But, she wondered, had she made a new friend?

Then she looked into the back of the station wagon. The two carriers were empty. And back at Wild Paws there was another empty animal crate. In the last few days, the black bear cubs had found a new home. And so had Tuffy.

Many hellos. Many goodbyes.

Sweet and sour.

Max leaned back against the car seat. She closed her eyes.

Sweet and sour. People who worked to rehabilitate wild animals probably always had to live with a little of that feeling.

Max smiled. Maybe she could get used to it after all.

Black Bear Information Sheet

❖ Black bears can be found in all Canadian provinces and territories, except Prince Edward Island; in the majority of the U.S. states and in northern Mexico. Black bears are not always black. They can be light, medium or dark brown, blond or cinnamon. The Kermode bear or "Spirit Bear" is a black bear with white fur. It is found in the Yukon and rain forests of British Columbia. In Alaska, some black bears are pale blue! They are called "glacier bears."

❖ Black bears are omnivorous. They eat insects, especially ants, as well as fruits, nuts, acorns, grasses, roots and other types of vegetation. They sometimes will eat fawns and moose calves. Black bears on the coasts feed on salmon.

❖ Bears are very intelligent and have an excellent memory. They have extremely sharp senses of hearing and smell.

❖ Black bears make grunting sounds when they are relaxed. When they are scared, they make a loud blowing sound. At times, they may mumble, moan, squeak or roar. Cubs sometimes whimper.

🐾 Black bears can stand up on their hind legs for extended periods of time. They can also sit down on their rear with their upper body off the ground.

🐾 Male bears are called boars, and females are called sows. Babies are cubs. Except for mother bears and cubs, black bears usually live alone.

🐾 Black bears are dormant for periods during the winter. This lets them survive the winters without large amounts of food. When they are dormant, they do not eat, drink or urinate. Their temperature drops a little, and their breathing slows.

🐾 During dormancy, females give birth to a litter of one to five cubs. (Two cubs is average.) Cubs are born in January or early February. They weigh between 225 and 450 grams at birth. They are blind and toothless, and covered with fine hair. The mother bear cleans them with her tongue and keeps them warm. She puts them in a good position to nurse – and then goes back to sleep!

❧ Bears leave their dens in the spring. Cubs are weaned around six months old, but usually stay with their mother for a year and a half.

❧ Black bears are great at climbing, and climb trees to escape danger. Sometimes they sleep in the crotch of a tree.